Darren Thompson

The Bugligs

www.olympiapublishers.com
OLYMPIA PAPERBACK EDITION

A CIP catalogue record for this title is
available from the British Library.

ISBN: 978-1-83934-385-8

This is a work of fiction.
Names, characters, places and incidents originate from the writer's imagination. Any
resemblance to actual persons, living or dead, is purely coincidental.

First Published in 2023

Olympia Publishers
Tallis House
2 Tallis Street
London
EC4Y 0AB

Printed in Great Britain

Dedication

Dedicated to my two amazing granddaughters Tiffany and Caitlyn Love you both zillions x

There was a slight chill in the air, no sound, you could hear a pin drop.

The forest was not usually like this. Daddy Buglig knew danger was close, he was always very cautious when leaving the family home, which was in a large wood,

Deep down under the ground, it was snug and warm, and more importantly, safe. Bugligs were very small creatures, they had big black eyes with very, very good eyesight. Their ears were set pretty close to their face, yet they had good hearing. Their noses were quite round with hairy nostrils, their bodies were covered in a rough thick hair to keep them warm, they didn't need to wear clothes.

Daddy Buglig was on his daily search for food, he used his highly developed hearing to detect the movement of bugs and worms in the undergrowth.

The big fat stag Beatles were his favourite food. Deep fried they were exceptionally crunchy the way Mummy Buglig cooks them. His mouth was watering at the thought of them.

As if out of nowhere there was the sound of heavy footsteps crunching through the fallen leaves.

Daddy Buglig knew he had to hide, and hide quickly. He looked around desperately, looking to find a safe hiding place, somewhere the ground crunchers wouldn't find him,

They were grumpy loud creatures, they had big ears which gave them fantastic hearing, they had small eyes which stuck out rather a lot, their eyesight was not very good. Their bodies had very dark hair, they were very solid and strong, they would eat birds, rabbits and squirrels but their favourite food, the food they loved the most, above all else was buglig ice-cream.

Grandpa Ground Cruncher hadn't tasted buglig ice-cream for a long, long time. He would stoop down very low to the ground, his ears would wiggle as they analysed the various sounds. A branch snapping, a bird swooping past, a butterfly enjoying his day, but what was that other sound? Could it be the opportunity to taste buglig ice cream again?

His nose flared as he took a long slow sniff, his eyes, although not very good, scouring the ground for movement. He saw it, just to his left there was most definitely movement.

He pounced like a wild tiger hunting its prey, his hand stretched out and grasped the ground, he felt movement, he had lunch.

His hand moved closer to his eyes, very cautiously so as not to let it escape, he opened his grip just enough to see what his lunch might be.

A mouse, he had caught a mouse. Oh well not what he had hoped for, but certainly not the worse either. Roast mouse with oak leaf sauce was actually rather tasty.

He turned and made his way home, back to the hollowed out tree he called home. Some ground crunchers lived high up the tree trunk, some lower down, but they all lived in hollowed out trees.

No one knows what their homes look like inside. No one had been inside one and lived to talk about it.

No one wanted to know what they were like, almost everyone was scared of the ground crunchers.

Daddy Bugligs heart was pounding in his chest, he thought the ground cruncher had him for sure, he had felt his hand brush past his ear as he hid under the leaves as he grabbed the mouse that was out minding his own business.

He dared not move for several minutes in case the ground cruncher was tricking him and was hiding, waiting for him to return.

At last, he summoned up the courage to move and resumed his hunt for dinner of his own.

He pushed his hands deep under the leaves feeling for any

movement or warmth.

After several attempts, he had enough bugs to feed his family, all tucked up in the small bag he wore attached to his fat tummy. It was time to go home before it got too dark.

It wasn't long before he was at the entrance of their family home under the ground. He looked around to make sure nothing was watching so as to not give away the whereabouts of their home.

He lifted a rectangular hatch that was covered with leaves to make it invisible when closed and quickly entered inside.

Daddy Buglig had built stairs out of twigs bound together with twine.

There were twenty steps to get down, each pushed into the mud, it took a lot of digging to build a buglig home.

It was a massive feeling of relief to be home again, he felt relaxed and safe.

"Daddy, is that you?" called Caitlyn Buglig, she was his youngest daughter.

"Yes, of course, it is me. Did you think I was a ground cruncher come to eat you up?" said Daddy Buglig.

"Haha, Daddy, you are so funny, no ground cruncher would fit in our home."

Daddy handed her his belly bag. "Take this to Mummy, we will eat well tonight." Caitlyn took the bag to Mummy who called for Tiffany, her big sister, to help her prepare the dinner.

It wasn't long before they were all sat around the family table Daddy Buglig had built using twigs with love and care, he was very proud of his table.

Mummy Buglig carried in dinner on a large leaf, it smelled very yummy. After eating Daddy Buglig thanked Mummy for their very yummy dinner.

"Bedtime now," said Mummy.

"OK," said Caitlyn, "come on, Tiffany, bet I am faster than you getting to bed."

"No you're not," said Tiffany, already starting to run to their room.

Caitlyn and Tiffany shared a bedroom, they had made their own decorations using various dried out flower petals which they had pressed into the mud walls,

"Good night, Daddy, good night, Mummy," they both said together.

"Goodnight, girls," said Mummy and Daddy.

Daddy Buglig woke suddenly and sat upright, something didn't feel right.

He got up and left Mummy asleep and went to check the girls were OK. They were both asleep and Tiffany was snoring, as usual.

Daddy smiled and went to check the rest of their home. Everything seemed to be OK, maybe he had had a bad dream. He went up the stairs to the front door, carefully he lifted the hatch just a small bit so he could look outside. He looked left, he looked right, he looked straight on, it was raining and it made a very relaxing sound as the rain hit the ground.

Daddy cautiously opened the hatch just enough to be able to get out the family home and looked all around. It seemed safe, he made his way towards the lake which was pretty close to their home, looking and listening out for danger as he walked.

The ground shook underneath him and he fell hitting his nose, the ground shook again as a very large ground cruncher ran towards him, his footsteps making the ground shake as his feet hit the ground.

Daddy caught movement out of the corner of his eye, quickly, he got up and dived for cover just as a very large hand grabbed out towards him. He felt the sharp tip of the ground crunchers fingernail just catch the tip of his ear.

He dived deep into a pile of leaves and froze, not daring to move, he tried to control his breathing so as to make as little noise as possible.

"I know you are here, I saw you, I can still smell you," said the ground cruncher. Daddy dared not speak, he lay still as can be hoping the ground cruncher would not find him.

Daddy was very, very scared, he knew that if he moved he would be dinner for the ground cruncher.

The ground cruncher pushed his large hands through the leaves in circular movements in an attempt to find the buglig he had seen.

He was very close, Daddy heard the hand swoop past him, it was getting closer each time as the ground cruncher pushed his hands deep into the leaves, first the left hand then the right.

Daddy felt his foot being touched. "Got you," shouted the ground cruncher as his hand grasped at Daddy. Daddy was lifted up out of the leaves and was very, very scared. His only hope was that the ground cruncher didn't have a very good grip on him and he would be able to wriggle free.

He wriggled and wriggled as hard and as fast as he could. But the ground cruncher had him and was not letting go. Daddy was desperately thinking about how he could escape, the ground cruncher was already walking towards his home. The ground cruncher reached the tree and reached out to open the wide bark door. Daddy remembered his daddy telling him what to do if he found himself in just such a situation.

He did just as his daddy had told him, he bit the ground crunchers finger as hard as he could and left his teeth in the ground crunchers finger. It felt hairy and tasted disgusting but he wasn't going to let go, he sunk his teeth harder into the finger. Suddenly the ground cruncher yelled out in pain and he released his grasp on the buglig. Daddy felt himself falling and could see the ground getting closer and closer, he prepared himself for the landing and looked to see what the ground cruncher was doing.

The ground cruncher was sucking his finger, it was very sore, the ground cruncher was very, very angry.

How dare the buglig bite him, how dare he ruin the lovely dinner he had planned for himself.

Daddy buglig landed on the ground, his leg hurt but he knew he was not out of danger yet. He ran as fast as he could away from the tree, he saw a hollowed out tree in front of him and ran towards it as fast as he could.

The ground cruncher had recovered. Despite still having a sore finger, he wasn't going to give up on the chance of buglig dinner just yet.

He ran after the buglig and, as he was much bigger with much longer legs, he was catching up to Daddy very quickly.

Daddy did not hesitate, he rushed straight into the hollow tree, it was dark inside, Daddy couldn't see a thing.

The ground cruncher was outside the tree, the hollowed out tree was too small for him to fit inside.

The ground cruncher reached his hand into the hole, grabbing around inside the tree. Daddy backed up as far as he could until he could go no further and his back was on the far side of the tree. Daddy could hear the swooping sound of the ground crunchers hand trying to grasp him. This went on for several minutes.

Gradually Daddy's eyes got used to the dark. He could see shadows and the movement of the ground crunchers hand trying to get him.

As Daddy looked around he could see markings on the inside of the tree. He was not sure what they were initially, but as his eyes got used to the dark, it became clearer and clearer.

He could see a ladder carved into the side of the tree, someone had made a ladder. Daddy wasn't sure who had made it but he didn't have time to worry about that.

The ground crunchers hand was coming closer and was about to get him, he edged sideways towards the ladder, he reached it and started to climb upwards.

He climbed higher and higher, not sure where he was going or where he would end up. The ground cruncher was still laying on the floor by the tree, pushing his arm as far inside the hole as he could, swooping his hand around inside feeling all around.

Daddy reached the top of the ladder there was a ledge which he stepped onto. He could see light at the end of the ledge. He cautiously walked to the end and could see that it led to another small hole in the tree. He could fit through quite easily and found himself on a branch outside the tree.

He looked all around, there was a bird on a nearby branch watching him, they stared at each other for a while then the bird flew off.

Daddy looked down and could see the ground cruncher still sprawled on the floor, his arm still inside the tree.

"Come back, come back, buglig, I wanna eat you all up," the ground cruncher was muttering to himself.

Daddy Buglig sat on the branch for a few minutes to catch his breath, his heart was still beating very fast.

Several minutes had passed, his heart was now beating normally again. The ground cruncher was now sitting by the tree, maybe he was going to give up and go away, then he placed his face right up close to the hole and made a very loud and long growling sound inside,

The growl echoed right up inside the tree and Daddy felt the hairs on his back prick up, he was very scared.

Mummy Buglig woke up to find Daddy was not in bed. She got up and looked around the family home for him, Tiffany was still asleep but Caitlyn had just woke up.

“Where is Daddy?” Caitlyn asked.

"I don't know, maybe he has gone outside," said Mummy. Caitlyn ran towards the door and started climbing up the ladder.

"No, Caitlyn, don't go outside, it's not safe," shouted Mummy. But Caitlyn wasn't listening, she wanted Daddy.

She quickly reached the top of the stairs and didn't hesitate, she opened the hatch and went outside.

She looked around and headed towards the lake where Daddy would collect water. 'Maybe Daddy is there,' she thought to herself.

"Daddy, Daddy, where are you?" she shouted. She forgot that Mummy and Daddy had told her to keep quiet whenever she was outside. All she knew was that she wanted Daddy.

She got closer and closer to the lake. Daddy could hear her from high up on the tree, he knew that if he could hear her, so could the ground cruncher. "No, Caitlyn, go home now," shouted Daddy.

The ground cruncher had heard Caitlyn but his eyes were not very good, so he hadn't seen her yet.

He stood up and took a deep breath in, sniffing the air and turning his head trying to find out which direction the sound had come from.

Caitlyn spotted the ground cruncher and started shaking in fear, Daddy had told her about them but she hadn't actually seen one before. He was very big and ugly and very, very scary. She turned and started to run back to the family home as fast as she could.

The ground cruncher was still sniffing the air, turning his head all around. Then, despite his eye sight not being very good, he caught movement out of the corner of his eye. He didn't know what it was but it was small, this meant it was good for dinner.

The ground cruncher started in the direction he had seen movement, he couldn't see anything yet but it smelt like buglig.

'How is that possible,' he thought, 'how did he get out the tree?

I was there the whole time.'

He thought Daddy had got out of the tree and wasn't going to let him get away this time.

Daddy was still high up the tree, he looked around, there was a twine rope just down from the branch he was on. He ran and jumped and caught the rope and started to slide down it. He reached the end of the rope but was still quite high up the tree. There was another branch that had another hole back inside the tree. Daddy dropped of the rope onto the branch and headed straight back inside the tree.

Caitlyn was getting closer to the family home with the ground cruncher catching up with her.

"Come back," bellowed the ground cruncher!

Caitlyn was running faster then she had ever run before, she was very very scared. She didn't want to end up being dinner for such an ugly ground cruncher.

Daddy's eyes were getting used to the dark, he spotted another rope leading down, he did not hesitate. He leapt onto the rope and started to slide down, his hands were burning from the rope as he slid down faster and faster. He didn't care, he wanted to save Caitlyn from the ground cruncher.

He reached the ground and ran out the hollow tree after the ground cruncher, he wasn't sure what he was going to do yet, but he was going to save Caitlyn even if it meant the ground cruncher catching him instead.

Caitlyn reached the hatch and lifted it and got inside as fast as possible. "Mummy, Mummy, help me help me," she yelled.

Mummy rushed to see what was going on. Caitlyn reached the bottom of the stairs and hugged mummy, she was shaking, she was so scared.

Daddy saw her enter the family home, but so did the ground cruncher. "Ha, I have got you now, there is nowhere for you to run.

I will dig down and eat you," yelled the ground cruncher.

Mummy heard this and knew exactly what they must do, she shouted for Tiffany and grasped Caitlyn's hand.

"Quick, this way," she exclaimed.

Tiffany came out of the bedroom. "What's going on?" she said.

"No time to explain, we have to get out," Mummy said.

"But the ground cruncher is at the top, how are we going to get out?" said Caitlyn.

"Quick this way," said Mummy, running towards the end of a passage. She shoved the wall and mud fell off revealing a hidden door.

"Wait," said Caitlyn and broke free from Mummy's hand. She ran back to their bedroom and grabbed teddy, then ran back to Mummy.

Mummy opened the door and pushed them both inside then she followed and closed the door behind them.

It was very dark, both the girls were scared. "Quickly, girls, go as fast as you can," said Mummy.

All three stumbled along in the dark as fast as they could, the passageway was dark and damp and seemed to go on forever.

The ground cruncher was at the entrance to the family home, he started jumping up and down all around the area around the door. Mud and bits of branches were falling from the ceiling, it wouldn't be long before the roof collapsed and the ground breaker would be inside.

Daddy stopped running, watching what the ground cruncher was doing. 'I hope Mummy remembers the emergency plan,' he thought. 'I will see if I can distract him.' He set off in a different direction, watching the ground cruncher.

He yelled, "Hey, you ugly beast, I'm over here, I'm over here."

The ground cruncher looked at Daddy in the distance. "I will get you another day, I have one trapped right here, and I'm going to eat it," he snarled, and jumped up and down even harder.

The roof was shaking and bits were falling everywhere. Daddy carried on running until he came to a clearing next to a hollow log, it had a very distinctive prickly bramble by the side of it.

He entered inside the log, had a quick look around to make sure there were no rats. Although rats won't want to eat him, they are not the friendliest of animals.

Mummy and the girls continued running along the passage, it seemed to go on and on forever, Daddy sat inside the log waiting.

Suddenly, the ground cruncher started falling, the roof was strong, but could not put up with the ground breaker constantly jumping on it. He found himself in a deep, deep hole surrounded by mud.

He was in the family home, as soon as he realized what had happened he started lifting mud up and throwing it up outside, quickly looking all around for signs of movement, he didn't want the buglig or bugligs to escape.

Mummy heard the roof cave in but kept on going with the girls. 'It can't be much further,' she thought!

The ground cruncher had thrown the dining table up and out and was desperately looking around for bugligs. The scent of bugligs was very strong, and there was more than one, maybe even more than two.

Daddy was still waiting in the log very worried that Mummy and the girls had been caught.

At last Mummy had reached the end of the passage, there was a ladder made of twigs leading straight up, it felt old and damp. Mummy hoped it would still be strong and not break as they climbed it.

"Go, girls, as fast as you can, I am right behind you," said Mummy.

The girls didn't hesitate, Caitlyn put teddy in her mouth and held his ear with her teeth, she needed both hands to climb the ladder.

Up, up, up, up they all went, it seemed a long way.

The ground cruncher had cleared most of the mud and had discovered the escape door. He ripped it out the wall but could see nothing down the long damp passage. He could not fit inside so made his way back to the area that was once a front room.

He climbed his way back out and looked all around the hole that was the family home, maybe the bugligs would be close, maybe he still would have buglig for dinner.

Daddy could hear a tap tap tapping sound, it appeared to be getting closer. Daddy stared at the floor right in the middle of the log, it was if he was waiting for something.

Then there was a creaking sound, the floor of the log was moving, a hatch came up out of nowhere and the girls and Mummy entered the log.

Daddy was overcome with happiness, Mummy had remembered the emergency plan after all.

They all hugged each other, but they weren't out of danger just yet.

Daddy looked out the edge of the log, in the distance he could see the ground cruncher. "Listen very carefully, the ground cruncher is still close. They are pretty fast so we can't outrun them. We need to leave this log, it won't be safe here for very long. The ground crunchers have very good noses and if one comes close to this log, he will know we are inside. We need to go," said Daddy.

"I'm scared," said Caitlyn.

"Yes, we all are," said Mummy, "but Daddy is right, it isn't safe to stay here. We have a long way to go before it's safe but there is a place we can stay until tomorrow, it will be dark soon. It's started getting dark already," said Mummy

"Right , I'm pretty sure that if we sneak in that direction " daddy said pointing to a very large old tree,the girls nodded, " not much further, there is a buglig hideaway for bugligs that are caught out late at night, its very old, I've not been there for a long time but I'm sure it will still be there".Said Daddy.

"Caitlyn, you lead the way with Tiffany. And no matter what you see or hear,don't look back and keep going " said daddy

"   We will be right behind you" said mummy

They waited a few seconds to build their courage up, daddy looked out to see where the ground cruncher was, he was still by the remains of the family home.

"Right ,let's go " said daddy, "and be as quiet as you possibly can, no talking, " said daddy

They all went to the end of the log, clutching her Teddy ,Caitlyn led the way to the large tree, the rest all followed her as quietly, and quickly as they could.

Daddy kept looking back to see if the ground cruncher had seen them, So far so good. It looked very promising they were almost there, then there was an almighty roar.

The ground cruncher had caught their scent in the wind and was heading in their direction .

"Quickly,go as fast as you can, I will go another way go try to distract him, do not stop until you are safe inside" said daddy .

Mummy nodded and continued onwards with the girls, Daddy turned and ran towards the ground cruncher yelling at him " Here I am,You can't catch me you grumpy ugly monster"

The ground cruncher looked directly at daddy and licked his lips and pointing right at daddy, he then pointed inside his mouth several times.

Daddy knew exactly what he meant, daddy was going to be dinner, but not if he could help it.

Mummy and the girls continued towards the big tree, they were getting closer, it won't be long now, but what about daddy, thought mummy.

The ground cruncher was gaining on daddy, then daddy tripped over a branch and fell straight to the floor!

Mummy and the girls had reached the big tree, right next to it was a hidden hatch, mummy quickly cleared the leaves from the top of it, lifted it and ushered the girls inside, as soon as they were inside there was a staircase made the same way that daddy had built, they started going down .

"What about daddy" said Tiffany and Caitlyn at the same time.

"Daddy is very clever, I hope he can out wit the ground cruncher" said mummy As daddy lay on the ground, the ground cruncher loomed above him

"Got you now, you can't outrun me. I can almost taste you" said the ground cruncher, his mouth watering in anticipation of his buglig dinner.

He reached out his massive hand to grab daddy, he felt daddy's body as he grasped his hand around him.

Daddy was very very scared, he didn't know what to do this time, the ground cruncher won't fall for the biting trick a second time.

As daddy was lifted up into the air, there was a strange swooping noise, daddy found himself falling down and laying on the ground.

The ground cruncher was gone,

He looked all around, as he did a feather fell to the ground.

Daddy looked up, there was a massive owl,He had the ground cruncher firmly in his claws

Daddy was amazed, he thought that the biggest, ugliest ground cruncher he had ever seen, was going to enjoy him for lunch.

He sat still for a few minutes getting over the shock of what had just happened.

He quickly made his way back to the big tree, looking out for owls, he had heard of them before, but had not actually seen one until today.

It wasn't long before he was going into the hatch and down the stairs after mummy and the girls" I'm coming, I'm safe " he called out.

Mummy and the girls had reached the bottom ,they looked around.

There were a couple of doors, mummy opened one, there was a lot of dust, it was a pretty big room, bigger than the family home.

Around the sides were several beds, all made of twigs, there was a very long table in the centre with chairs all around, set into the walls at various places were very small lamps, giving just enough, light to see by.

Mummy opened the second door, it was exactly the same as the first but it had been cleaned recently, mummy called the girls " we will stay here tonight.

"What about daddy " said Caitlyn, just then daddy came in through the door, " I'm here" daddy said .

They all hugged each other for quite a while, after which daddy explained how he had fell over and thought that he was going to be lunch, then the ground cruncher was taken away by an owl.

They were all amazed by his story, none of them had seen an owl before.

On the table was a bowl of dried worms, they were not the girls favourite but they were all very hungry, so ate them without a fuss .

The girls picked a bed and decided to both sleep in the same one, it had been a long long scary day.

It wasn't long before they were both snoozing and Tiffany was once again snoring, Caitlyn had her teddy tucked up tight and close.

Daddy and mummy sat at the table, there was a small lamp in the centre. Mummy had tears rolling down her cheeks," our home is gone" said mummy,

"yes, but we will go to granddads house, it is very very big, there will be plenty of room for all of us, I can build us all new beds", said daddy,Mummy nodded.

"Come on mummy, we need to get some rest, there is still quite a way to go tomorrow", said daddy.

Mummy agreed and they chose beds and went to sleep.

Daddy woke up a few times thinking the ground cruncher had found them, but it was just him dreaming.

Caitlyn was the first to wake up, she looked around, at first she forgot what had happened, Tiffany was next to her in the bed, I remember, she thought.

She went over to daddy and hugged him, he had been very brave.

It wasn't long before they were all awake, "Right girls, are you ready to visit Nanny and Granddad, we will be staying with them, whilst we decide what to do" said daddy

"Yes yes yes," said both girls excitedly.

They had a few more dried worms each to get them set for the journey, they weren't sure what there would be to eat on the way.

They all climbed up the long staircase, daddy peered outside the hatch to ensure it was safe, then they all ventured out.

"Lets go," said daddy, leading the way,

"Keep your eyes open for danger and be quiet" said mummy

Both girls looked at mummy, both nodded, they did not want to see another ground cruncher.

As they walked along in the woods, they saw several small birds looking for worms for their breakfast.

A deer and its babies were also out for an early morning walk.

Suddenly the sky lit up quickly followed by an almighty bang that echoed all around the trees.

The sky opened up and a torrent of rain came crashing down, the rain bounced of the ground as it hit, " Quick this way we need to get to cover" said daddy.

Daddy led the way to a tree that had fallen in a big storm several years before.

The ground quickly changed into mud with slippery leaves on the surface, it became difficult to walk on, let alone run.

Tiffany slipped and was about to hit the floor when mummy grabbed her arm pulling her up in one smooth motion.

The shock on Tiffany's face turned to a smile as she looked up at mummy, "Quickly girls, follow Daddy." Said mummy

Daddy continued towards the tree as the rain continued to crash down, due to their size, it was very frightening, it would be the equivalent of balls of rain like tennis balls to humans.

A rabbit darted straight at them unaware they were even there, its back leg just clipped Caitlin and threw her high upwards, Daddy ran towards her reaching out as he ran, as she fell back down Daddy jumped and caught her in mid air, he pulled her towards himself and as he fell downward , twisted his body so that he took the impact and Caitlyn landed on top of him.

"Are you hurt?" Daddy asked, Caitlyn looked him and burst into tears. "Are you hurt?" repeated Daddy.

" I don't think so" she replied

Daddy quickly got up and carried her the remaining distance to the fallen tree. Mummy and Tiffany were right behind him.

They climbed right under the fallen tree, it was ideal cover from the rain, another streak of light crossed the sky, "What's happening daddy" ,asked Tiffany.

" It's only a storm, it will end soon, we will wait here until it does. Said Daddy.

It seemed to go on for ages, Caitlyn cuddled up to mummy, " I don't like it mummy" she said

"Your safe here", Said mummy., Brushing the rain out from Caitlyn's fur. Eventually, the rain began to ease off, it was time to continue their journey.

It was difficult to walk as the ground was so wet, the leaves would move under their feet. Both the girls held on tightly to mummy and daddy. They didn't want to fall over.

they carried on for what seemed an eternity then Caitlyn started moaning "I'm tired, my feet hurt, I'm hungry " she said, " yes I could do with a rest myself",said mummy

Daddy nodded, " not much further and we can rest at the next hideaway";he said. Mummy smiled at him and nodded in agreement.

HATCH

After about another ten minutes or so and just as Caitlyn was going to give up and just sit down, Daddy pointed to a tree not far ahead, "We are there",He said.

"At last, thought Tiffany, just to the left of the tree, hidden with twigs and leaves just as before, was the hatch.

Daddy cautiously lifted it up and peeked inside, "Come on, " he said,leading the way in. Down the stairs they all went, this one seemed to have been built very recently.

Just as they reached the bottom, they all heard a noise, some-one,or something was down there.

There was only one door this time, it opened and a very old buglig peered round it. "Welcome, welcome, I've not seen another buglig for a long long time, come on, come

in. I am just keeping the hideaway in good order, the stairs were in need of replacing so I

have been staying here for a while" said the old buglig.

" I am an Elder , we keep these hideaways clean and ensure there is food at the table ,come and rest and eat. " he said

Daddy led the way into the room, it wasn't as big as before, it had lights around the sides, with a couple of beds and a table in the middle.

The girls did not need much encouragement, they climbed onto chairs by the table and grabbed a handful of dried worms and rammed them into their mouths, they were very very hungry .

The girls then both climbed into the nearest bed, it wasn't long before they were both asleep.

Daddy and mummy sat with the Elder and told him all about their adventures , and why they were there.

He listened and every now and then nodded .

When they had finally finished the elder said" you certainly have had some excitement these last few days, you better get a good nights rest to prepare for your continued adventure, don't worry, you will be safe here"

Daddy and mummy agreed, heading towards the nearest bed.

It wasn't long before both were sound asleep , they were both exhausted from the whole adventure.

The Elder continued to sit at the table eating a dry worm every now and then as he thought about what Daddy had told him.

After a while, he went to bed himself.

The next morning the Elder had already been out to find breakfast, when everyone had awakened ,he had a wonderful breakfast all ready for them of the finest beetles .

Both the girls rushed up to the table, they were really looking forward to the crunchy beetles.

The only sound that could be heard was the crunching of beetles , The girls both had a smile on their face as they enjoyed breakfast.

There was also a fresh brew of oak leave tea, this was mummy's favourite. Daddy preferred just water but he drank the tea without complaint.

Daddy thanked the Elder for all he had done for them, but it was time for them to continue on their journey.

The Elder nodded in agreement,

"Caitlyn don't forget your teddy" mummy said.

Caitlyn went back to the bed and grabbed it. Smiling as she came back to mummy.

At last ,everyone was ready to go, they all said goodbye to the Elder and made their way back to the door.

They all followed Daddy up the stairs, everyone was feeling a bit excited but also scared at the same time.

Daddy opened the hatch just enougn to see outside ,

"Wait here " he said as he went outside. He had a good look around then opened the hatch " come on ,its safe" he said.

Everyone ventured outside ,the girls had a good look round,

the sky had a few clouds and it was no longer raining, the ground was still wet, but not as slippery as it was last night.

”Come on ,lets go ” said Daddy leading the way

Caitlyn held his hand tightly so as not to fall. Teddy in her other hand.

Tiffany was quite happy to walk behind them, but she kept looking back in case there was a ground cruncher after them.

The birds were singing in the trees, they saw a pair of squirrels jumping between branches.

The ground squelched under their feet it felt cool in between their toes

Both girls were feeling excited, Daddy kept looking all around and listening to ensure their safety.

Several minutes passed as they made their way to their new home .

Daddy noticed that the birds were no longer singing , something was wrong , he looked all around signalled for everyone to keep still and remain very quiet .

Mummy was scared , the girls were scared .

Suddenly there was a a strange animal bounding towards them ,it was getting closer very quickly, it had large flappy ears which went up and down as it ran , very large white teeth and four legs.

It was heading straight for them Daddy pushed the girls out the way just as it reached them , they sprawled onto the floor and lay as still as possible, the monster hadn't seen them ,it continued straight on past them and it's neck reached out and grabbed something

It turned and came back towards them, it had something red in its mouth "Wolfie, Wolfie " a voice called out in the distance .

The monster ran in the direction of the voice with the red thing still in its mouth. Both girls were very shaken and hugged close to Daddy

" what was that " they both asked

" I think that was a dog, the humans have them , it was very scary but I'm sure it didn't even know we were there" said Daddy

"Is it coming back " ? Asked Caitlyn

" I don't think so , but Let's get going " said Daddy

They all started walking again somewhat shaken by the dog.

Caitlyn was especially nervous constantly looking around whilst holding both Daddy's hand and teddy .

Eventually they reached a patch of ground that had a circle of oak trees in the middle . "Now girls ,our new home is very close , Grandad spent a very long time building this

home and it is very well hidden, the entrance is in that oak tree there, the biggest one "

said Daddy.

Both girls had excitement in their eyes as they neared the tree.

Daddy had a final look round to ensure they were not being

watched before entering into the tree closely followed by Mummy and the girls.

Once they were inside the tree Daddy went to the far side inside the trunk and pulled on a twine rope a couple of times .

Several minutes later a hatch lifted in the floor and a face appeared "This is Grumpy Granddad "said Daddy .

Grumpy Granddad said "Hello" and beckoned them into the hatch.

They all followed him and just as at their old home was a staircase made out of twigs leading downwards,

It was fairly dark to start with, but as they got further down , there were lamps set into the sides just bright enough to enable them to see where they were going.

It was a very long staircase, so they knew that it was a very long way underground. When they reached the bottom , there was a passageway leading off into 2 directions "This way" said Grumpy Granddad

They followed as he opened a door which lead into a large room .

In the centre was a large table made in the same style that Daddy had made theirs. There was chairs around it ,

Lamps were set deep back into the walls around the edges. There were 3 other doors around the room .

"That one is the escape route , if anything happens go straight through that door and follow the passage

It will lead you up into a tree a safe distance from the entrance tree that you came in ,stay inside of this tree until everyone is inside." Said Grumpy Granddad .

They all nodded in understanding.

"That door is mine and Nanny's room " Said Grumpy Granddad pointing at the next door.

" That door will be your room and the door inside that room

leads to another room for Daddy and Mummy , we will have to make you beds tomorrow , for tonight Nanny is collecting dry leaves which you can sleep on, she should be back soon, " Said Grumpy Granddad

"On the table there are some dried worms and water " before Grumpy Granddad had even finished saying this both the girls were at the table giggling as they munched on the dried worms.

Grumpy Granddad smiled , something he does not normally do .

Nanny emerged through the emergency exit with a big bag of dried leaves and a big smile on her face.

Both girls rushed over to her and gave her a big hug. "Hello girls , I'm sure you will like living here " Said Nanny "Umm" muttered Grumpy Grandad.

After the girls had finished eating , Nanny lead them to their room to lay the leaves out ready for them to go to bed.

There were lamps around the sides in all the rooms which made it feel very friendly and homely .

It wasn't long before they were both asleep , cuddled up together with Caitlyn's teddy by her side.

Nanny watched them for a few minutes just to ensure that they were settled down ok. Daddy was sitting,up at the table with Mummy and Grumpy Granddad telling him all

about their last few days.

" I will make some oak leaf tea " Said Nanny,

That archway there , leads to the cellar where supply's and food is stored .

"There is a place to wash in there as well " Said Nanny pointing to the far side of the large room they were in.

Nanny returned with the oak leaf tea ,Daddy and Grumpy Granddad were still talking about their last few days.

"Im Really tired Daddy, I am going to go to bed " Said

Mummy

“ yes it has been an eventful last few days, that sounds like a good idea , good night Grumpy Granddad and Nanny” Said Daddy.

It wasn’t long before it was just Grumpy Granddad left on his own sitting at the table.

The next morning , both girls woke up , they were a bit confused as to where they were, but they soon remembered.

“What is that noise” Said Caitlyn , grabbing her teddy for comfort, “Daddy where are you ?“ Said Caitlyn .

Very quickly Daddy appeared at the door “What’s the matter” Said Daddy

There was a loud vibrating noise

“ Wait there , I’ll be right back” Said Daddy as he went to investigate the noise. Mummy appeared in the room, they all waited anxiously , it wasn’t long before they

could hear Daddy laughing

“ it’s ok girls, come here “ Daddy called They rushed to the front room,

Grumpy Granddad was laying on the floor asleep and snoring very loudly. Mummy and Nanny both walked into the room , Nanny smiled “ he often snores like that” she said

“Wow, look “ Said Caitlyn excitedly pointing to two beds both made identically from twigs woven together except one had Caitlyn and one had Tiffany’s name made out of very small twigs on the headboard of the beds .

“Wow that’s so cool “ Said Tiffany. Grumpy Grandad woke up

Caitlyn and Tiffany jumped onto him shouting “Thankyou Thankyou our beds are amazing”

Grumpy Granddad had spent most of the night making their new beds before he had fallen asleep on the floor next to them .

Both the girls were looking forward to sleeping in their new beds.

They all sat around the table eating dried worms for breakfast, Tiffany and Caitlyn tried the oak leaf tea.

Caitlyn's face screwed up in disgust, " that is not nice at all " she said.

Grumpy Grandad and nanny both laughed, " may be you should stick to plain water" nanny said.

Caitlyn nodded in agreement , reaching out for the jug of water. " I rather like the oak leaf tea "said Tiffany.

Mummy and Daddy smiled.

They spend the whole day inside their new home talking and planning on how they would decorate their new home with leaves , just like they had in their old room.

Soon it was time for bed.

"Goodnight Nanny , good night Grumpy Grandad " said both girls together, Mummy and Daddy took the girls to their room,

It wasn't long before both girls were fast asleep, Tiffany gently snoring just as usual. Both were dreaming of the new adventures they had yet to enjoy.

About the Author

I originally started writing this in my teens but for a reason I am not sure of never finished it. I rewrote it approximately a year or so ago. I love films of all genres, I have been married twice, I work in fresh foods, I love gadgets.